PAT HUTCHINS

King Henry's Palace

GREENWILLOW BOOKS
New York

Printed in the United States of America
First Edition   10 9 8 7 6 5 4 3 2 1

Library of Congress Cataloging in Publication Data

Hutchins, Pat, (date)
King Henry's palace.
Summary: Three short stories about a
pleasant palace where a nice king lives
happily with his cook, gardener, servants,
and guards, who wish only to please him.
[1. Kings, queens, rulers, etc.–Fiction.
2. Palaces–Fiction. 3. Household employees–
Fiction]   I. Title.
PZ7.H96165Ki   1983   [E]   83-1453
ISBN 0-688-02294-4
ISBN 0-688-02295-2 (lib. bdg.)

FOR CLAIRE

Contents

King Henry's Palace

King Henry was a very nice king.

The cook liked him and cooked lovely
dinners for him.

The gardener liked him and grew
beautiful plants for him.

The servants liked him and made sure the
palace was always neat and tidy,

and the guards liked him and took turns
guarding the palace for him.

The king had such a nice, happy little
palace that wicked King Boris, who lived
in a nasty, unhappy palace, wanted it for
himself.

13

"Oh dear!" said King Henry when he
saw wicked King Boris marching toward
the palace. "We have only ten guards,
and he has hundreds!"

14

"Aha!" said wicked King Boris. "We have
hundreds of guards and he has only ten!"

But King Henry, who was clever, asked
his guards to bring their flags and
drums to the palace walls.

16

Then he asked the servants to bring the
pipes and swords.

Then he asked the gardener to bring the
pistols while he put the cannons in place.

"Look," said wicked King Boris, who was
not so clever. "Ten guards with flags!"

19

"But ten more with drums,"
said the guards,
"and ten more with pipes,

and ten more with swords,
and ten more with pistols,

and ten more with cannons–there must
be hundreds of them!" And wicked
King Boris and his men ran away.

22

King Henry laughed. "Hundreds of
guards frightened by my ten," he said.

23

King Henry's Birthday

It was King Henry's birthday and the
cook decided to bake a special cake for
him. He took a bowl of cherries from the
pantry.

"They look like nice cherries," said the
gardener, tasting one.

"Very good cherries," said the servants.

"Excellent cherries," said the soldiers,
who were taking turns to guard the
palace.

"They were," said the cook, looking at
the empty bowl.

He brought a dish of nuts out of the
pantry.
"They look like nice nuts," said the
gardener, tasting one.

31

"Very good nuts," said the servants.

"Excellent nuts," said the guards, who
were taking turns to guard the palace.

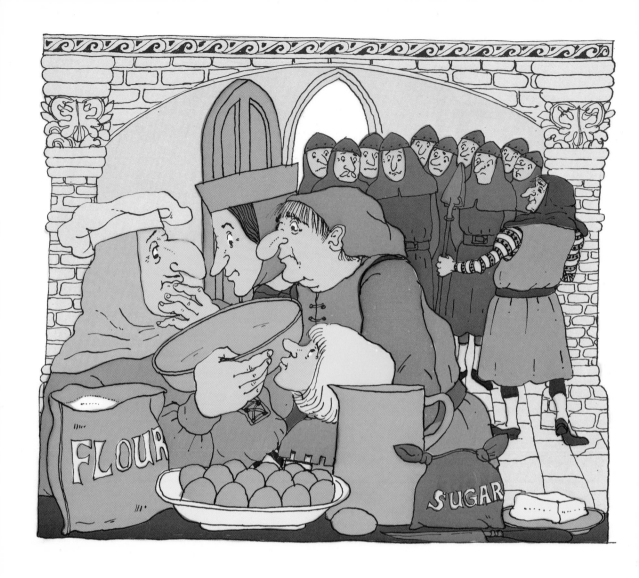

"They were," said the cook, looking at
  the empty dish.
"I'd better get back to my gardening,"
  said the gardener.

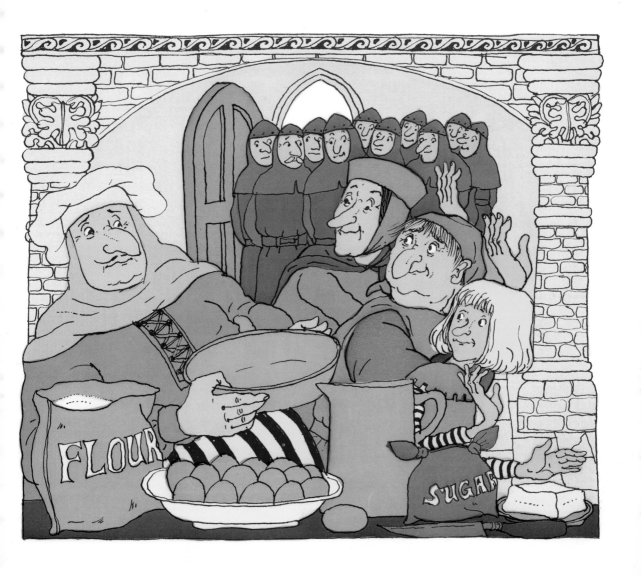

"And we'd better get back to our cleaning
and tidying," said the servants.

"And we'd better take our turn at
guarding the palace," said the guards.

"Oh dear," said the cook. "All I have left
is flour, sugar, milk, and eggs."
So he put the cake tin back in the
cupboard, and took out a frying pan.

"Pancakes," said King Henry. "My
favorites! Everyone must have one."

38

"Wonderful pancakes," said the king.

"Very nice pancakes," said the gardener.

"Very good pancakes," said the servants.

"Excellent pancakes," said the guards,
who were taking turns to guard the
palace.

"They were," said the cook, looking at
the empty plate.

41

King Henry's Christmas Present

It was Christmas Eve.

The gardener, who was very good at growing beautiful plants, but not very good at woodwork, decided to make King Henry a garden seat.

"We'll help," said the guards, who were
very good at taking turns to guard the
palace, but not very good at measuring.

45

"We'll help," said the servants, who were
very good at keeping the palace neat and
tidy, but not very good at sawing wood.

46

"I'll help," said the cook, who was very
good at cooking, but not very good
at hammering nails.

"Perhaps it will look better in the
garden," said the gardener. So they
carried it into the garden.

48

"Oh!" said King Henry when he saw it.
"Thank you," he said, as he sat down
  on it.
"Such a surprise," he said, as it collapsed.

"Wonderful!" he shouted, as it slid down
the hill. "A sled! I've always wanted a
sled! Everyone must have a turn."

And while the cook took his turn on the
sled, the gardener carried a Christmas
tree into the palace.

And while the soldiers took their turns,

the servants set the table and decorated the tree.

And while the servants took their
turns on the sled, the cook prepared
a marvelous feast.

And after the gardener had his turn,

they all went in to eat it.